Geronimo Stilton

Queen

Duchess

March Hare

Mad Hatter

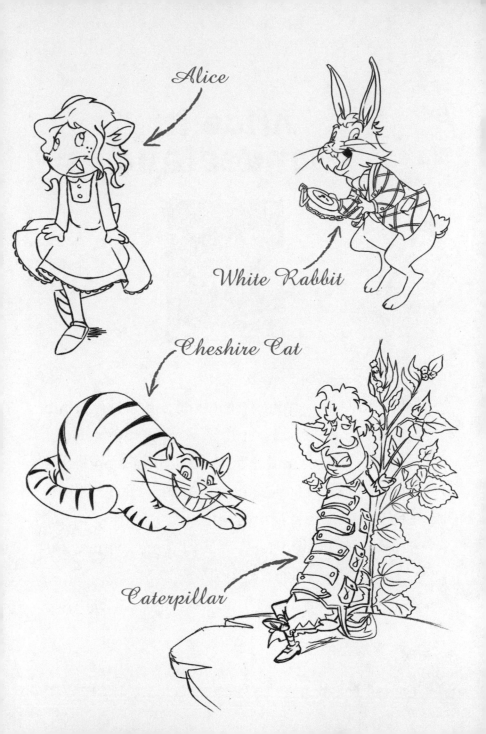

Alice

White Rabbit

Cheshire Cat

Caterpillar

Alice in Wonderland

Dear rodent readers,

My love for great stories began a long time ago, when I was still a young mouselet. I spent hours and hours reading wonderful books! They took me on fantastic adventures to mysterious, faraway lands. Reading made my imagination soar — and it made me want to become a writer, too!

So I thought I'd share one of my very favorite tales with you — a great literary mousterpiece. This is the story of Alice, a curious young mouselet. One warm summer afternoon, she spots a strange White Rabbit in a field . . . and she decides to follow him! That's just the beginning of her fabumouse journey to Wonderland, a world full of unusual characters and unforgettable adventures. Let's join her!

Geronimo Stilton

Published by Scholastic Inc., *Publishers since 1920*, 557 Broadway, New York, NY 10012.

SCHOLASTIC and associated logos are trademarks and/or registered trademarks of Scholastic Inc.

Stilton is the name of a famous English cheese. It is a registered trademark of the Stilton Cheese Makers' Association. For more information, go to www.stiltoncheese.com.

ISBN 978-1-338-05293-0

Original text by Lewis Carroll
Adapted by Geronimo Stilton
Original title *Alice nel Paese delle Meraviglie*
Cover by Flavio Ferron
Illustrations by Andrea Denegri (pencils and inks) and Christian Aliprandi (color)
Graphics by Simona Gargantini and Jole Montalbano, with Yuko Egusa

Special thanks to Shannon Penney
Translated by Emily Clement
Interior design by Kevin Callahan / BNGO Books

10 9 8 7 6 5 4 3 2 1   17 18 19 20 21

First printing, January 2017

Geronimo Stilton

Alice in Wonderland

Based on the novel
by Lewis Carroll

Scholastic Inc.

Down the Rabbit Hole

Alice was tired of sitting on the riverbank in the English countryside near her house. Cheese and crackers, there was nothing to do! Her older sister was nearby, reading from a **book** without any illustrations, and Alice was mousetastically bored.

"I could make a daisy crown," she said halfheartedly. But it was *hot* as melted mozzarella outside, and Alice felt lazy. She was just about to get her paws in gear to start picking flowers when a huge White Rabbit wearing a waistcoat **darted** in front of her! He seemed to be in an enormouse hurry.

"Oh, heavens! I'm late!" the Rabbit **cried**, stopping only a few steps from Alice's snout. Alice watched as the Rabbit pulled a pocket watch from his waistcoat, checked it, and bolted away. Holey cheese, how *strange*! Where could he be going in such a hurry?

Curious, Alice ran after him. She crossed the field next to the river and scurried as fast as her paws would take her. She didn't want to lose sight of the White Rabbit!

Alice reached the edge of the field just in time to **GLIMPSE** the White Rabbit jumping into a big hole just beyond a hedge. Where could he be going? Alice knew she really shouldn't follow him. Her sister would worry about her and wonder where she had **GONE**. But Alice was so bored

and longing for an ADVENTURE. She promised herself she would come right back after she saw where the White Rabbit had gone. Alice had made up her mind. Without another thought, she jumped into the hole, too! WHOOOOOOSH!

Drink Me!

The **RABBIT HOLE** must have been really deep, because Alice had plenty of time to look around as she *fell*.

Cheese niblets, what a strange hole! **Hanging** on the walls were wardrobes, paintings, shelves, playing cards, maps, and all sorts of odd things!

"Who knows how far I'm falling?" Alice wondered **aLOuD**. "I'm probably getting close to the center of the earth. I bet I'm already at a latitude and longitude very far from home. Squeeeeak!"

Alice always tried to use **BIG WORDS** to show that she was a smart young mouselet — even if she wasn't totally sure what they meant! Finally, tired from thinking so hard and from running after the White Rabbit, she **fell fast asleep**.

But then right in the middle of her nap . . . **BOOM!**

Alice finally hit the bottom of the hole! She landed in a pile of dry leaves. Moldy mozzarella, what luck—not only was she unharmed, but her fur was hardly even ruffled! As soon as she got to her paws, she spotted the White Rabbit in the distance, hopping away down a **long** tunnel.

Alice got her tail in gear and hurried after him. But when she reached the end of the tunnel, the White Rabbit had disappeared. ℛats!

Alice was now in a long hallway. Chandeliers hung from

the ceiling, and closed doors lined the walls. The mouselet paced back and forth, twisting her tail.

"What now?" she wondered with a SIGH.

Then she saw a small three-legged table she hadn't noticed before. On the table was a little golden key. "Maybe this key opens one of the closed doors!" Alice squeaked hopefully.

She walked down the hall, trying the key in all the locks, but none of the doors opened. Alice was about to lose hope when she spotted a tiny door hidden behind a curtain. She tried the key in the keyhole . . . and it was a perfect fit! She could have squeaked with joy!

Alice crouched down in front of the open door and PEEKED through. She could see a narrow hallway with a beautiful garden at the end.

"Rat-munching rattlesnakes!" Alice cried. "I'm too **BiG** to get through there!"

In fact, the doorway was so small that the mouselet's **HEAD** wouldn't have even fit through it!

"Oh, if only I were smaller!" she said with a sigh. "I wish I could go through that door . . ."

Not knowing what else to do, Alice locked the tiny door again and returned the key to the table. She peered around, trying to figure out her next move. Then, right under her snout, she saw a tiny bottle with a tag that read *Drink Me!*

Alice examined the bottle suspiciously. "Hmmm. I really shouldn't drink from a mysterious bottle," she said, "especially if it's labeled *Poison*."

But this bottle wasn't labeled POISON, so

Drink Me!

Alice decided to drink it anyway. She had nothing else to do, and she didn't want to stand around in that hallway forever!

"Oh, it's DELICIOUS!" she squeaked.

"It tastes like a cream cheese tart, a mozzarella milkshake, a double-cheese pizza, Parmesan pancakes, and Swiss fondue . . . all in one!"

Sip by sip, Alice drank the whole bottle!

Curiouser and Curiouser!

When she was finished drinking, a very odd feeling came over Alice.

"How strange!" she murmured. "It almost feels like I'm . . . shrinking!"

In fact, as she had sipped from the bottle, Alice had **shrunk** little by little. Before long, she was only ten inches tall!

Alice jumped for joy. Now she was small enough to fit through the little door and reach the garden! But when she *rushed* over to the door, she realized that she had left the key on the table. Rats! Now that she was so TINY, she couldn't reach it!

"Oh no!" she **groaned**. "What a terrible turn of bad luck!"

She plopped down on the ground and BURST into tears. Now what?

Between sobs, she noticed that a small glass box had appeared under the table. How strange — she was sure it hadn't been there earlier!

Curious, Alice opened it. Inside was a small chocolate cake. Written in icing across the top were the words *Eat me!*

"All right, cake," she said, "I'll eat you! On one paw, if you make me grow, I'll be able to reach the key. On the other paw, if you make me smaller, I'll be able to **SLIP** under the door." A grin stretched across her snout. "Either way, I'll get to that beautiful garden!"

Alice took a bite of the little cake and waited to see if she would GROW or shrink.

Curiouser and Curiouser!

But nothing happened. So she ate another bite, and another, and another. Soon she had eaten the entire thing. Squeak! The moment she finished, another odd feeling came over her.

"Curiouser and curiouser!" she cried in shock. "Now I'm *stretching* out!"

A Sea of Tears!

Alice LOOKED down at her feet, but they were so far away she could barely see them.

"Good-bye, feet!" she said. "I'll miss you, way down there!"

As Alice tried to stand up, she ran into a bigger problem. Her head hit the ceiling! Rancid ricotta—now she was almost ten feet tall! She quickly grabbed the golden key that she had left on the table.

But holey cheese—now she was way too ENORMOUSE to fit through the little door!

A Sea of Tears!

Disappointed and frustrated, Alice felt tears rolling down her snout again. A few moments later, she heard a shuffling noise in the distance. Who was coming?

The White Rabbit raced down the hall, holding a pair of white gloves in one paw and a large fan in the other.

"Oh, the Duchess! The Duchess!" the Rabbit mumbled to himself. "She'll be **FURIOUS** that I'm so late!"

Alice needed someone to help her, and the White Rabbit was the only creature in sight. So she squeaked to get his attention. "Excuse me, Mr. Rabbit!"

As soon as he noticed her, the White Rabbit jumped back in surprise. His fan and gloves fell to the ground, and he hopped away quickly. Rats!

A Sea of Tears!

Alice picked up the gloves and fan and waved them around in dismay. "Everything is mousetastically **strange** here! To think that I was bored out of my fur at home not so long ago . . ."

Lost in thought, she looked down and realized that she had put on one of the Rabbit's **white gloves**.

"Wait a minute!" she cried. "How can such a small glove fit on my paw? I must have **shrunk** again!"

She scrambled to her paws and stood next to the table to measure herself. Cheese niblets—she was only about a foot and a half tall now. And she was still getting **smaller**!

When she realized what was happening, Alice threw the fan and the gloves to the ground—and she immediately

stopped shrinking! "Thundering cattails!" she **SQUEAKED**. "I've never been so small in my life!"

Whooshhhh!

A wave rolled in, and she was suddenly immersed in an enormouse **SEA** of her own tears! Cheese and crackers, what was she going to do now?

Help Me, Mr. Fish!

As she **BOBBeD** in the waves, Alice moaned, "Oh, I wish I hadn't cried so much when I was big!"

Just then she felt the water moving behind her. She turned, frightened out of her fur! Not far away, a huge Fish was splashing around peacefully.

Alice paused, twirling her whiskers with one paw. Was she really going to approach a gigantic fish, especially one she'd never met? But so many strange things had happened that day already! She had to try.

"Please help me, Mr. Fish!" she cried. "Do you have any idea how to get out of this water? I'm getting so tired! I'm not a fabumouse swimmer, like you."

The Fish looked at her CURIOUSLY but didn't reply.

Maybe he's afraid, Alice thought.

"You don't have to worry, Mr. Fish," she went on. "I'm just a little mouselet, not something terrifying like a **cat**!"

Hearing that word, the fish dove down into the water, trembling.

Alice sighed. Poor thing! Even if he was *gigantic*, he was clearly as afraid of cats as she was.

"Oh, Mr. Fish, forgive me!" she squeaked. "I shouldn't have mentioned cats."

"No, you shouldn't have!" he REPLIED, opening his mouth for the first time. "Cats just want to eat me."

Alice couldn't help feeling ***relieved***. At least the Fish spoke her language!

"You and I have that in common," she said. "Cats are so **frightening**, with their sharp claws and pointy teeth. But, luckily, dogs aren't quite as bad, especially for a Fish!"

The Fish swam away again, **shuddering**.

Alice held her head in her paws. "Moldy mozzarella, look what I've done! Wait a minute, Mr. Fish!" she begged. "Come back, please! I won't talk about cats or dogs ever again — *rodent's honor*. I need your help!" The Fish cautiously swam up next to her.

"Will you lead me out of this **WATER**?" Alice squeaked desperately.

"Very well, young mouselet — I'll show you to the shore," the Fish agreed.

Help Me, Mr. Fish!

As they moved slowly through the **waves**, they were joined by a Duck, a Dodo, a Lory, an Eagle, and many other different kinds of birds.

Before long, the whole group reached a **beach**. Alice was thrilled to be back on dry land and gratefully waved good-bye to the Fish. But the birds' feathers were soaking wet, and they were all very **UNHAPPY**. Alice's fur was wet, too, and her whiskers wobbled as she shivered.

They had to find a way to dry off, and fast—otherwise, someone could catch a **fUR-RaiSiNG** cold!

Each of them made suggestions for how to dry off, and Alice **eagerly** joined in the debate. After a heated discussion, the Eagle *raised* his wings to quiet the crowd.

"Everyone sit down and listen to me!" he ordered. "I will dry you off with something very . . . **dry**!"

With that, he began to make a very long speech. "A long time ago—no, a long, long, long (and when I say long, I mean **LOOOOOOOONG**) time ago . . ."

Someone **coughed** politely.

The Eagle's speech was definitely **dry** and boring—but it wasn't helping to dry any feathers or fur!

The Eagle continued: "It was a length of time that was—how should I say this?—**looooong** . . ."

His speech seemed as though it would never end. Then, **suddenly**, he stopped and turned to face Alice. "Is everything okay, my dear?"

"Well," the mouselet replied, "I'm still SOAKED from the ends of my ears to the tip of my tail!"

"In that case," the Dodo intervened, "I have a solution!"

Everyone Wins!

"I propose that we stop sitting around," the Dodo continued. "It's time for more **drastic measures**!"

The other birds blinked, perplexed.

"The best way to get dry is by running a race!" the Dodo said.

He grabbed a stick and traced the race route in the dirt. Alice noted that it looked like a kind of **crooked** circle.

"The exact shape DOESN'T MATTER," the Dodo clarified.

All the birds lined up randomly on the course. As soon as the Dodo squawked, "Ready, set, go!" they all **started** to run. They stopped whenever they wanted, and they zigzagged in every possible direction. Alice followed their lead, more CONFUSED than a mouse in a maze. What a strange race!

After about a half hour of running, everyone felt nice and dry.

"The race is finished!" the Dodo declared.

The other birds crowded around him, still breathing heavily as they smoothed their feathers.

"Well, who's the WiNNer?"

"Who came in first?"

The Dodo thought about it for a moment, with one wingtip held to his beak.

"Well, the winner is . . . everyone!" he finally declared.

"Everyone won, and therefore everyone will receive a prize."

"**OOOOOOOOH!**" the runners cried.

"Who's giving out the Prizes?" someone asked.

The Dodo pointed to Alice. "*She* will give them out, naturally."

The birds all crowded AROUND the mouselet, shouting and squawking.

"Prizes! Prizes!"

"Where are our prizes?"

Alice didn't know what to do. She didn't have any prizes! She rummaged through her pockets. Fabumouse—she found some cheese-flavored hard candies! The wrappers had kept the salt water from spoiling them, so she carefully distributed the candies to the birds.

She had exactly one piece of candy for

each winner, but there wasn't one left for her.

"That's not right!" the Eagle **protested**. "She needs a prize, too!"

"That's true," the Dodo said *seriously*. He turned back to Alice. "What else do you have in your pockets, mouselet?"

Alice dug into her pockets again, but she found only one thing.

"Just a thimble, unfortunately," she squeaked with a sigh.

But the Dodo didn't seem disappointed at all! He delicately took the thimble, inviting everyone to come closer.

"I beg you to accept this fine thimble as a **PRIZE**," the Dodo said solemnly, handing Alice her own thimble.

Everyone Wins!

The birds all applauded enthusiastically.

Holey cheese, how **SiLLY**! Alice wanted to laugh, but the birds seemed so serious that she accepted her prize with a little curtsy instead.

A Loooooong Tale

Once everyone had eaten their candies, Alice realized that the Fish was still **WATCHING** them from the water. She sat on the sand nearby and said, "I understand why you don't like cats. For the love of cheese, neither do I! But what do you have against dogs?"

"Ah!" the Fish said with a sigh, raising his eyes to the sky. "That's a loooooong tale!"

With that, the Fish began to tell his story. As he spoke, Alice imagined his words *curling* up into the air, forming the shape of a big fish tail . . .

"One day, a dog spotted a fish in a river and said, 'I'll steal your scales!' The poor fish said, 'My dear doggy, why must you steal my scales?' 'Because your scales reflect the sun, and it's burning my eyes!' replied the ferocious dog.

"Hey, you're not listening!" the Fish sputtered all of a sudden, SCOLDING Alice. "What's going on in that cheesebrain of yours?"

"Oh, I'm sorry!" she murmured, blushing. "I was imagining the words of your story in the shape of a tail . . ."

Annoyed, the Fish mumbled something and swam away. Before Alice could twitch a whisker, he had disappeared.

"Oh no!" Alice moaned. "I'm making one enormouse MESS after another today! If only I could get the Fish to listen to me.

I've met some dogs that are quite friendly!"

"Dogs?" the Lory piped up suddenly. **"WHERE?"**

Alice waved a paw. "Oh, there are no dogs here. At least, I don't think there are." She paused thoughtfully. "I haven't seen any, but then again this is such a **strange** place I suppose there could be dogs or cats or any number of **fur-raising** things just around the corner . . ."

Alice's words ruffled the birds' feathers! Some of them flew away immediately, **terrified**. Others squawked quick excuses for leaving:

"Um, I have a sore throat!"

"And I have a cold! **Achoo!**"

"Er, I have an appointment. Yes, I have to be somewhere important **right away**."

"I have to go check on my eggs!"

A Loooooong Tale

Before she knew it, Alice found herself **alone** again. This time, she couldn't help the tears that trickled down her snout. Holey cheese, what was she going to do now?

I'm Late! I'm Late! I'm Late!

Alice was still **CRYING** when she heard steps moving toward her. She wiped her eyes with her paws, and there was the White Rabbit again!

Cheesy cream puffs! She was sure she had **lost** him.

The Rabbit was sifting through the dirt carefully, as if he were looking for something.

"I'm late! I'm late! I'm late!" he mumbled, walking right past Alice. "Oh, where could they be? They must have fallen around here somewhere . . ."

Alice remembered the **FAN** and white gloves that the Rabbit had lost in the hall, so she started to look for them, too.

Maybe if she could help him, the White Rabbit would help her! But everything had changed after Alice swam through the sea of tears. The hall seemed to have completely **disappeared**!

As Alice scoured the ground, the Rabbit finally noticed her.

"Mary Ann!" he yelled **GROUCHILY**. "What do you think you're doing? Go to my house and bring me a pair of gloves and a fan. *Get your tail in gear!*"

Alice was so startled that she scurried quickly in the direction the Rabbit had pointed, through the nearby woods.

Mary Ann? she thought. *Cheese niblets, he must have confused me with someone else. Oh, well! Let's hope I can find some gloves and a* **fan** *— if I can even find his house . . .*

I'm Late! I'm Late! I'm Late!

Before she could finish her thought, she found herself standing in front of a charming little two-story house. A BRASS plaque hanging on the door read W. RABBIT.

Alice was in such a rush, she didn't even bother to KNOCK. She darted inside and up the stairs, looking for the White Rabbit's closet.

"How strange to be pawing around a Rabbit's house!" she said to herself, peering into the different rooms.

After a quick tour, she entered a tidy room with a small table under the window. On top of the table were a fan and several pairs of white gloves. Fabumouse!

Alice didn't waste any time. She grabbed the fan and a pair of gloves, and was

about to **leave** the room when her **eyes** fell on another little bottle on the tabletop.

Every time I drink from one of these tiny bottles, she reflected, *something* INTERESTING *happens. Who knows what could happen this time! Maybe I will grow big again. Oh, I hope so! I'm* tired *of being so tiny!*

The young mouselet couldn't resist!

Alice had only drunk half the bottle when she felt her head pressing against the ceiling! She had to bow down to keep from lifting the **roof** right off the house.

"Oh, rats!" she cried. "I said **BiG**, but I didn't mean **this big**!"

Alice continued to grow, and grow, and grow! Soon she had to crouch down on the floor. How *uncomfortable*!

One of her arms popped out through an

45

open window, and one of her feet squeezed into the fireplace.

"Thundering cattails, what have I gotten myself into?" she squeaked.

When she finally stopped **growing**, she heard a voice coming from the front door of the house. Alice was all ears — who could it be?

Bill the Lizard

Alice heard someone *screeching*, "Mary Ann! Where are those gloves?"

She recognized the White Rabbit's voice, and heard him run up the front steps in great **Leaps**.

The mouselet was so afraid of how he'd react when he saw her there, she completely forgot that she was now one hundred times **bigger** than him! Holey cheese!

The Rabbit soon reached the door to the room where Alice crouched, stuffed like a bellyful of cheese pizza. He tried to **open** the door but couldn't — Alice's elbow was pushed up against it!

"Hey! What's going on?" the Rabbit

called. "I'll come in through the window if I have to!"

Alarmed, Alice waited to hear the Rabbit's steps under the window. Then, she waved the arm that was sticking out the window and tried to gently GRAB the Rabbit in her paw. Before she could reach him, she heard a shout, quickly followed by the crash of **breaking** glass. Moldy mozzarella, the Rabbit must have fallen on something!

"Pat!" the Rabbit yelled. "Get me out of here!"

Alice heard another loud crash.

"Now tell me, Pat," the Rabbit continued, "what's coming out of that window?"

"An arm, sir!" a voice replied steadily.

"But don't you see how BIG it is?" the Rabbit said. He was getting very agitated. "It fills the whole window!"

"Sure," Pat confirmed. "But it's still an arm."

"Well, there's no reason for it to be *blocking* my window," the Rabbit declared. "Get it out of there!"

A *long* silence followed. Alice had to wait and see what happened! Before long, she heard the squeaky wheels of a cart, and many **CONFUSED** voices all talking at once.

"Where's the ladder? Bill! Bill, bring the ladder!"

"Bill, grab that rope and **CLIMB** onto the roof!"

"Now go down the chimney, Bill!"

"Oh, cheese niblets!" Alice muttered, **ANNOYED**. "Why does Bill have to do everything? Bill, whoever you are, I wouldn't want to be in your paws!"

Alice waited for Bill to slide **down** the chimney. When he landed on her paw in the fireplace, she gave him a little **KICK** to send him back outside! She didn't want him to get stuck, and there was no way for him to get past her paw.

Outside, she heard a COMMOTION.

"Bill, old boy, what happened?"

Bill mumbled something in shock and then *fainted*.

Just then a shower of pebbles rained on Alice through the window that wasn't **blocked** by her arm. Strangely, as soon as the pebbles touched the floor, they turned into little **cheesecakes**!

"Crusty cat litter—I could eat one!" she cried. "I can't possibly grow any more, so these cheesecakes will surely make me **smaller**!"

As soon as Alice swallowed one of the tasty cheesecakes, she began to shrink. What a relief! Once she was small enough to fit through the door, she rushed out of the house.

As soon as she stepped outside, she saw the White Rabbit standing with some other animals, including a VERY PALE lizard held up by two guinea pigs. *The lizard must be poor Bill!* she realized.

Careful not to be spotted, Alice scampered into the woods as fast as her paws would take her.

Whoooo Arrrre Yoooou?

Once she was far away from the White Rabbit's house, Alice gave a **squeak of relief**. "I barely got away!" she said with a sigh.

But what was she going to do next? She was so small now she was only an inch tall!

"First of all," she decided, "I have to get to the right **SiZe** to reach the garden I saw at the end of the hallway. Then I must figure out **HOW** to get there. What a fabumouse plan!"

And it was! Too bad Alice didn't have the slightest **idea** of how to make it happen.

"Let's see," she thought aloud. "How can I

make myself bigger — but not enormouse —
again? Surely I have to eat or drink
something . . . but what?"

Alice examined all the flowers and blades
of grass nearby. Then her eyes fell on a
large mushroom. It was almost the same
size as her! Alice stretched up on her tiptoes
and peeked over the top.

Holey cheese — her eyes met those of
a large Caterpillar! He was sitting on the
mushroom cap with his legs crossed, and
he didn't seem to be bothered by
her . . . or by anything else.

The Caterpillar and Alice
stared SILENTLY at each other
for a few minutes. Finally, the
Caterpillar stretched toward
her and asked in a slow, sleepy
voice, "Whoooo arrrre yoooou?"

"Well, actually . . . I don't quite know, sir!" Alice admitted.

"What do you mean? Explain yourself," the Caterpillar urged her. "If I do not understand, you must make me understand!"

"Unfortunately, sir, I can't make you understand who I am," Alice tried to explain, "because I don't know if I'm me anymore! Changing size so many times has left me mousetastically confused, you know!"

"No, I don't know at all," the Caterpillar replied calmly.

"Well, you don't know now," Alice said thoughtfully. "But when you eventually transform into a chrysalis and then into a butterfly, that will be a little strange for you, too, don't you think?"

"Not at all!" the Caterpillar replied shortly, shaking his head.

Alice felt like **tearing out** her fur. This conversation wasn't getting her anywhere, so she turned on her paws to **leave**.

Just then the Caterpillar started waving his little legs. "Wait! Wait! I must tell you something **very important!**"

Curious, Alice returned to the mushroom.

"What size would you like to be?" the Caterpillar asked.

"At least a little bigger than I am now," Alice said. "Really, one inch is a *ridiculous* height!"

The Caterpillar straightened up, irritated. He was exactly one inch tall! "Ridiculous?! It is an *excellent* height!"

"Oh, it's just not what I'm used to!" Alice said, trying to make up for offending him.

"Well, anyway," the Caterpillar added

with a great **yawn,** "one side will make you bigger, and the other will make you smaller."

One side of what? thought Alice, **confused**.

"Of the mushroom!" the Caterpillar shouted, as if the young mouselet had spoken **out loud**. She was so startled she nearly jumped out of her fur!

By the time she looked up again, the Caterpillar had **disappeared**.

Serpent! Serpent!

Alice examined the mushroom very carefully, trying to figure out which side would help her grow **bigger**.

Finally, she reached her arms as far around the mushroom cap as she could and broke off a piece with each paw. She took a tiny nibble from the piece in her right paw, to **SEE** what effect it would have.

BUMP!

Before she knew it, Alice felt something **smack** into her snout. Crusty cat litter — she had shrunk so fast that one of her feet had hit her own snout! **Ouch!**

She quickly munched on a **piece** of the mushroom from her left paw. "This should go better!" she squeaked, feeling her head rise **HIGH** into the air . . .

. . . a little too high!

Alice looked down and realized that her neck had STRETCHED out so much that it looked like a flower stem above a sea of green leaves.

"What's all that green stuff around my feet?" she wondered. "And where are my shoulders? I can't even see my poor paws! Cheese and crackers, what an enormouse disaster!"

Alice squinted, trying to see what was below her. Thundering cattails! She realized that her head was so high in the air that the leaves below were actually the **TOPS** of the trees! It was useless to try to bring her paws up to her head, so she tried to lower her head down to her paws. That's how she discovered that her **LONG** neck could easily bend in any direction, like a snake.

As she tested out different movements, a loud whistle made her fur stand on end.

Tweeeeeeeeeeeee!

"Serpent!" squawked a shrill voice.

Suddenly, a storm of **PECKING** beaks and **Fluttering** wings surrounded Alice's snout!

When the air cleared, Alice realized that the voice belonged to a LARGE Pigeon.

"Serpents, serpents — always serpents," the Pigeon said with a sigh. "It's **difficult** enough to sit on a nest of eggs, but now I also have to fight off serpents all the time!"

"I'm so sorry to have bothered you," Alice apologized. "But as you can **see**, I'm not a serpent."

Serpent! Serpent!

"Well, of course!" the Pigeon said. "So what are you, then?"

"I'm a mouse," Alice replied.

"A mouse, huh?" the Pigeon said dubiously. "And I bet you're going to tell me that you don't even eat eggs, right?"

"Well, I do love a good cheesy omelet," Alice admitted. She prided herself on being a very *HONEST* mouse! "But—"

The Pigeon cried, "See? Mouse or serpent, what DIFFERENCE does it make? You're still after my eggs! Get your tail out of here!"

Luckily, Alice still had the PIECES of mushroom in her paws. She took turns biting into them, first one then the other, until her neck was back to normal and she was her regular height again. *Whew*—what a mousetastic relief!

Serpent! Serpent!

She put the pieces of mushroom in her pocket and peered around. Now she found herself in a clearing just a few steps away from a large, fabumously *fancy* house!

Fish-Footman and Frog-Footman

As Alice studied the house, an elegant footman came out of the woods and headed toward the entrance.

Alice could tell that he was a footman from his uniform. But aside from that, he looked like a **BIG** fish! He carried an enormouse envelope.

The Fish-Footman knocked on the front door of the house. Another footman with a round face and two huge frog's **eyes** opened the door. Both of the footmen wore thick, **curly**, powdered wigs.

Quiet as a mouse, Alice crept closer.

The Fish-Footman waved the enormouse

envelope. "For the Duchess. An invitation to a croquet match on behalf of the Queen!"

As soon as he heard this, the Frog-Footman bowed his head **ceremoniously** and repeated the same phrases, just changing the order of the words slightly. "On behalf of the Queen. An invitation to a croquet match for the Duchess!"

Both *bowed* deeply in farewell. But as the Frog-Footman turned to go back inside, he realized that his wig had gotten *tangled* in the Fish-Footman's wig! Cheesy cream puffs, they looked so silly!

Alice couldn't help it — she burst out **LAUGHING**! She had to dart back into the woods until she calmed down, and so the footmen wouldn't hear her.

When Alice quietly returned to the front

of the house, the Fish-Footman had left. The Frog-Footman was sitting next to the front door, staring up at the sky.

Alice walked up to the door and looked at the Frog-Footman. He didn't move, so she lifted her paw and knocked on the door.

KNOCK, KNOCK, KNOCK!

"Oh, it's useless to knock," the Frog-Footman said. "I am the one who must open the door, but as you can **SEE**, I am outside with you. Plus, there's such a racket going on inside that it would be **IMPOSSIBLE** for anyone to hear you."

Cheese niblets, that was true! Alice could hear deafening noises coming from inside the house—shouts, sneezes, even the sound of plates breaking!

"But I would like to go inside," Alice

squeaked. "So what should I do?"

"Knocking would be useful if you were *inside*," the Frog-Footman said, **ignoring** Alice's question and getting lost in his own thoughts. "If you were inside and knocked, I could open the door and let you leave . . ."

Rancid ricotta, how **abSuRD**!

Just then the front door burst open. A large plate *flew* out, smacking the Frog-Footman in the head before slamming into a tree. Rats!

After a moment, Alice whispered, "Now may I go in?"

The Frog-Footman was too **dazed** to answer, so she decided to take matters into her own paws. She carefully stepped through the doorway . . .

The Duchess

The door led directly into a large kitchen full of smoke. The Duchess was seated on a stool in the middle of the room. (Alice recognized her because she looked truly fancy!) She held a newborn baby wrapped in blankets. Nearby, a tall cook vigorously stirred the soup in an ENORMOUSE cauldron.

Alice felt her nose twitch. Wait a cheese-loving minute — the gray cloud she had thought was smoke was actually pepper!

Because of all the pepper, the Duchess couldn't stop sneezing! The baby in her arms was sneezing and fidgeting, too.

The Duchess

The only ones in the kitchen who weren't sneezing were the cook and a fat **CAT** lying in front of the hearth.

Holey cheese — a cat! Alice froze.

Like everything in this land, the cat was very strange! His mouth spread into a half-moon **SMiLe** that stretched almost to his ears. The Cat stared at Alice, and his smile didn't waver for a second. Thundering cattails, how *unnerving*!

"Um, excuse me," she said to the Duchess, careful not to make any sudden movements in front of the cat. "Could you tell me why your **CAT** is smiling like that?"

"Because he's a Cheshire Cat," the Duchess replied shortly. "Of course!"

Alice was terrified of the strange cat, but she

couldn't help feeling **curious**, too.

"I didn't know that cats from Cheshire smiled like that," she confessed **POLITELY**. "Actually, I didn't know that cats could **smile** at all!"

"Oh, they **all** smile," the Duchess said.

"But I've never known one that has," Alice replied.

She wasn't **sure** that it was wise to contradict a Duchess, but she did want to learn more.

"You don't know much," the Duchess declared **crisply**. "That is the truth."

Alice twisted her tail in her paws. How rude! The Duchess hardly knew her!

Before Alice could think of what to say next, the cook took the cauldron of soup off the **fire**. Then she began to fling everything around her at the Duchess and the baby!

Alice nearly jumped out of her fur as pots, plates, and pans all flew through the air!

"Rotten rat's teeth!" Alice squeaked, holding up a paw to stop her. "Be **CAREFUL**, please!"

Meanwhile, the Duchess dodged the storm of flying objects as if it were nothing.

"If everyone just minded their own business," she told Alice seriously, dodging a saltshaker with a *graceful* leap, "I'm sure the earth would turn much more quickly!"

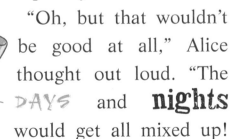

"Oh, but that wouldn't be good at all," Alice thought out loud. "The DAYS and **nights** would get all mixed up! The earth takes twenty-four hours to turn on its axis, so that means—"

The Duchess

"ENOUGH!" the Duchess interrupted. "I can't stand calculations and numbers!" Without warning, she handed the baby to Alice. "Here, you take it! I must go get ready to play croquet with the Queen."

Baby or Piglet?

Alice STRUGGLED to hold on to the baby. Rat-munching rattlesnakes — it wasn't just heavy, it kept wiggling its arms and legs in all different directions, too! "Can't you just stay still for a second?" she scolded.

When she finally managed to find a good way to hold it, the little one began to sneeze over and over again! Not knowing what else to do, Alice decided to take it outside for a walk. Once they were out in the fresh air, the baby finally stopped sneezing . . . and started SNORTING!

Worried, Alice carefully peeked under the blanket and examined the baby. It had round pink CHeeKS and a button NOSE that looked a little too much like a button. In fact, it looked more like a snout!

Even its EYES were unlike any baby's eyes she'd ever seen before!

"If you're intending to change into a piglet," Alice said seriously, "I can't take care of you anymore. You'll have to look after yourself!"

At that point, the poor thing started hiccupping. But the hiccups were actually loud, powerful snorts. There was no doubt about it—this really was a piglet! It didn't make sense to keep holding it like a baby, so Alice placed it delicately on the ground.

The piglet was delighted and trotted away into the woods.

"It may not have been the cutest baby,"

Alice said, "but it was a **FABUMOUSE** little piglet!"

As she reflected, Alice noticed a creature perched lazily on the branch of a nearby tree. She recognized it immediately.

"Chattering cheddar, what are **YOU** doing out here?" she squeaked in surprise.

Which Path Should I Take?

Alice carefully walked closer to the tree, where the Cheshire Cat had draped himself on one of the branches.

As soon as he saw Alice, the Cat's smile **stretched** even wider.

"Cheshire Cat," the young mouselet began, worried about what he might do next.

The Cat's smile grew even WIDER.

At least he's happy, Alice thought, feeling calmer.

"Cheshire Cat," she repeated, "which path should I take?"

"Well," replied the Cat, "that depends on where you want to go."

Alice shrugged. "That's the problem. I don't know!"

"Then it **DOESN'T MATTER** which path you take," the Cat pointed out.

"As long as the path goes somewhere," Alice added.

"Oh, it will surely go **SOMEWHERE**," the Cat said wisely. "You just have to walk for a **long** time."

Alice could see that he was right, but she wasn't sure how to reply. "Who lives around here?" she asked instead.

"In that direction," the Cat explained, waving his right paw, "lives the Mad Hatter. In **THAT** direction lives the March Hare.

You can visit one or the other of them, if you like."

Then the Cat

gave her another enormouse Smile. "See you at the Queen's croquet match!"

Alice was more **CONFUSED** than ever. The croquet match? But she hadn't been invited! And even if she had been invited, where was it being held? And **WHO** in the name of cheese was the Queen?

Before she could object, the Cat began to **slowly** disappear, starting with the tip of his tail. His smile was the last thing to go—it lingered long after the rest of him had vanished.

"Slimy Swiss balls!" Alice said. "How strange! He disappeared into thin air. I've seen cats without smiles many times. But I've never seen a smile without a cat!"

She waited under the tree for a few minutes to see if the Cheshire Cat would REAPPEAR. When he didn't, Alice

decided she had better shake a paw and get moving! She thought about it for a moment and then scampered in the direction of the March Hare's house, ready for whatever new *adventures* awaited her there . . .

A Truly Odd Tea Party!

Alice passed through a small **stretch** of woods and soon spotted a house that looked like it had rabbit ears (they were actually two chimneys) and a roof covered in *fur*.

"This must be the March Hare's house!" she squeaked.

The house was so fabumouse that Alice didn't want to approach it until she'd eaten another **Piece** of the mushroom. That way, she would be a bit taller and more respectable for a mouse.

Once she was a good size, she *nervously* headed for the front door.

"I hope the March Hare isn't as *grumpy*

as the Duchess!" she said to herself. "Maybe I should have gone to the Mad Hatter's house instead . . ."

But Alice wouldn't have to wait long to meet the **HATTER**!

In front of the Hare's house was a long table set for twenty guests, with teacups, **sugar bowls**, plates, pieces of bread, butter, and many other things. The March Hare was seated at one end, sipping his tea. Near him was a rodent wearing an enormouse hat — the Mad Hatter!

Between the two sat a **chubby** Dormouse, sleeping soundly. The Hare and the Hatter were using it as a pillow! They placed their elbows on its back while they chatted.

Rotten rat's teeth, what an uncomfortable

position for that Dormouse, Alice thought.

The table was very **LONG**, but the three creatures were all squished together at one end. How strange!

As soon as they spotted Alice, the March Hare and the Mad Hatter **LEAPED** to their paws.

"No room! No room!" they shouted, waving in alarm.

"But there's plenty of room!" Alice replied, sitting down in an armchair at the head of the enormouse table.

The Hare ran around the table and sat across from the Hatter. "Have a **CHEESY MILKSHAKE**," he suggested to Alice.

The young mouselet looked all along the table, but the only drink she saw was tea.

"Thank you very much, but I don't see any milkshakes," she said, confused.

"Actually," the Hare said matter-of-factly, "we don't have any."

Alice frowned. "Well, it's not very **polite** to offer me some if you don't have any!"

"And it's not very polite to sit down at a table without being invited!" the March Hare replied **disdainfully**.

"Oh, I'm sorry." Alice's cheeks turned as red as the sauce on a double-cheese pizza. "This table is so big that I —"

"Your hair is too **LONG**," the Mad Hatter interrupted. He had been **studying** Alice ever since she'd arrived!

"You shouldn't make personal comments like that," Alice scolded him. "It's not very **kind**!"

The Hatter's eyes widened, and he abruptly changed the subject.

"What do a **RAVEN** and a writing desk have in common?" he asked.

Fabumouse—finally something **fun**! Alice thought happily. She loved riddles!

Ridiculous Riddles

A *raven and a writing desk?* Alice reflected. *Let's see . . .*

The Mad Hatter and the March Hare watched her **nervously**.

"I think I can guess," Alice declared.

"Do you mean that you think you can answer the riddle?" the Hare asked.

"Yes!" Alice said with a nod. "I think I can guess the answer."

"Then you should say what you mean," the Hare continued.

"Yes, yes, that's what I meant to say," she replied. "That is, what I mean is the same thing you're saying!"

The Hatter's face darkened. "It's not the

same thing **at all**! That's like saying that 'I see what I'm eating' is the same as 'I'm eating what I see'!"

"Or that 'I like what they give me' is the same as 'They give me what I like,'" the Hare added.

The Dormouse muttered sleepily and tried to join in. "Or that 'I breathe when I sleep' is the same as 'I sleep when I breathe.'"

"But in your case, that *is* the same, my dear

Dormouse!" the Mad Hatter said with a laugh.

There wasn't much more to say after that, so the group fell silent. The March Hare and the Mad Hatter sipped their tea without offering Alice a drop.

Alice was having some **Difficulty** following the Mad Hatter's reasoning, so

instead she **tried** to remember what she had been thinking about writing desks and ravens. For the love of all things cheesy, she really wanted to solve that **ridiculous** riddle. Maybe then the March Hare and the Mad Hatter would offer her a cup of tea!

A Buttered Watch

The Mad Hatter was the first to break the silence. He pulled a large watch out of his pocket and started to examine it, looking worried. He even shook it and held it up to his ear a few times.

"What day of the month is it?" he finally asked Alice.

"It's the fourth," she REPLIED after thinking for a moment.

"Oh, I knew it," the Hatter said with a sigh. He shot an annoyed LOOK at the March Hare, who had returned to his seat on the other side of the Dormouse. "I told you that the butter wouldn't be good for the clockwork!"

"It was very good butter, though," the Hare replied CALMLY.

"Yes, but some crumbs ended up inside the watch, too!" the Hatter grumbled. "You shouldn't have used the bread KNIFE to spread it!"

The Hare took the watch and inspected it solemnly. Then he dipped it in his teacup. "Very good butter," he repeated.

Alice watched the whole exchange curiously. Cheese and tea cakes, these creatures were getting ODDER and ODDER by the minute!

"What an interesting watch," she said, looking at it more carefully. "It tells the day of the month, but it doesn't tell the TIME!"

"Why should it?" the Hatter asked. "Does your watch tell you what year it is?"

"Of course not," Alice replied quickly. "But that's because the year stays the same for a long time."

The Hatter shrugged. "Well, mine does the same thing for the hours of the day."

What in the world was he squeaking about?

"I don't really understand what you're saying," Alice confessed politely.

The Hatter didn't seem to care. "The Dormouse has fallen asleep again," he responded, pouring a few drops of **hot** tea on the creature's nose.

The Dormouse shook himself. "Zzz . . . of course, of course . . . zzzzz, I was just going to say the same thing, zzzzz . . ."

"Well!" cried the Hatter, turning back to Alice expectantly. "Have you finally solved the **riddle**?"

"No, I give up," Alice said, throwing her

paws in the air. "What's the answer?"

"Oh, I have no **iDea**," the Hatter confessed.

"Me neither! Me neither!" the Hare joined in, clapping his paws.

Alice sighed. She was **annoyed**. "Thundering cattails! You could find so many better ways to pass the time instead of wasting it on riddles without answers!"

The Mad Hatter crossed his arms. "If you knew **TIME** the way I do, young mouselet, you wouldn't say something like that. I bet he's never even spoken to you!"

"Maybe not," Alice replied with a shrug. "But when I study **MUSIC**, I have to beat the time."

The Hatter slapped his knee. "Ha! Time can't stand being beaten. But if you had a good relationship with him, you could ask the watch for whatever you want!"

Alice's **EYES** widened. This was truly marvemouse!

"Suppose that it's nine o'clock in the morning—time for school to start," the Hatter explained. "In this case, you could politely ask the watch to JUMP forward and go directly to lunchtime!"

"But I wouldn't be hungry first thing in the morning . . ." Alice said thoughtfully.

"Maybe not at first," the Hatter conceded. "But then you could stay at lunch until you were ready to eat!"

Alice's face lit up. "So is that what you've done? You decided to stop time at teatime?"

The Hatter shook his snout. "Oh, no, our case is very different! It all began last March. There was a grand concert put on for the Queen of Hearts," he explained. "I had to sing 'Twinkle, Twinkle'—you know, the song that goes,

'Twinkle, twinkle, little bat
How I wonder what you're at . . .'"

He performed a very unusual version of the song, warbling and **missing** almost every note.

Alice resisted the urge to clap her paws over her ears while she waited for the end of the performance!

The Hatter continued, "I was just about done with the first verse when the Queen started to **SCREAM**, 'He's keeping Time all wrong! Put him in prison!' And since then, as punishment, Time has made me stay at six o'clock."

A Buttered Watch

"Oh, now I understand!" Alice squeaked thoughtfully. "That's why there are so many places set at the table . . ."

The Hatter nodded. "Exactly—it's always time for tea, so we don't have time to wash the dishes. When they get DIRTY, we just change places."

"What a boring story!" the Hare muttered. "I think the Dormouse should tell us something new . . ."

The Chocolate Well

The Mad Hatter and the March Hare began to **SHAKE** the poor, sleepy Dormouse. "Wake up, Dormouse!"

The Dormouse **SLOOOOOWLY** opened his eyes, but he didn't twitch a whisker.

Losing patience, the Hare and Hatter pinched him. That seemed to ruffle his fur, and the Dormouse began to tell his tale. "Once, there were three sisters who lived in a **WELL**."

"What did they eat?" asked Alice.

"Chocolate!" the Dormouse replied, yawning.

"Chocolate?" Alice asked, **surprised**.

"Would you like another cup of tea?" the Hare interrupted, handing her a cup.

Alice looked **confused**. "Actually, I haven't had one yet. So how can I have another one?"

With a shrug, she accepted a cup of **tea** and some bread and butter. Then she turned back to the Dormouse. "Why did the three sisters live in a well?"

The Dormouse answered **SLEEPiLY**, "It was a chocolate well."

Alice tugged on her tail in exasperation. "But there's no such thing as a —"

"**Shhhhhh!**" the Mad Hatter and March Hare interrupted. "It's rude to interrupt!"

Alice threw her paws into the air. "Okay, I suppose that one chocolate well could exist **SOMEWHERE**," she cried.

"Who said anything about more than

one?" the Dormouse asked. "Anyway . . ."

"I want a clean cup!" the Hare announced, jumping up suddenly from his chair. "Let's all move to new spots at the table!"

With that, he slid into the next chair down. The Dormouse took his seat, the Hatter took the Dormouse's seat, and Alice reluctantly took the Hatter's seat. The only one who got a FRESH, clean cup was the Hare!

Alice looked down at her new place to

find that the Hatter had broken the **MILK** pitcher on the table. Thundering cattails, how inconsiderate! With her whiskers in a twist, Alice got to her paws and left without saying good-bye.

The Chocolate Well

After a few steps, she glanced back over her shoulder. The Ḥatter and the Hare hadn't even noticed she was gone! Instead, they were busy trying to **Stuff** the Dormouse into a teapot!

Alice sighed and headed into the woods. Paws down, that had been the *oddest* tea party she had ever been to!

White Roses, Red Roses

As she walked among the trees, Alice noticed that one of them had an enormouse hollow trunk with a door.

"Slimy Swiss balls, that's UNUSUAL!" she cried.

After taking a quick look around, she pushed open the door and went inside. How fabumouse! To her surprise, Alice found herself exactly in the same hall she had visited earlier, after her fall down the rabbit hole.

It was all there: the glass table, the golden key, the hallway—even the little door leading to that delightful garden!

White Roses, Red Roses

"This time, I must be careful not to MIX things up," Alice said to herself.

She grabbed the key and opened the door carefully. Then she took what was left of the mushroom pieces from her pocket and ate them until she was the right size to fit through the door. Finally, she ran down the hallway. *Holey cheese*—there was the garden she'd been looking for this whole time!

Alice peered around in admiration. Next to the entrance, she spotted a large rosebush. The **blooming** roses were white, but three gardeners were **painting** them red.

Why would they paint the roses? Alice wondered, moving **CLOSER** to get a better look.

The three gardeners looked very unusual.

Their bodies were **rectangular** and flat, and their arms and legs stuck out from the four corners. In fact, they looked just like three playing cards — a five, a seven, and a two of spades! Cheese niblets!

The trio seemed to be in a big *HURRY* to finish their work, but they were so clumsy that they were splattering paint everywhere *except* on the flowers!

"Watch out, Five! You're **splashing** everything in sight!"

"It's not my fault, Two! Seven keeps **poking** me and making me mess up!"

"Thanks so much, my dear Five! Always giving others a helping paw . . ."

Seven threw his paintbrush to the ground. Just then the trio noticed Alice standing nearby, and they all *bowed*.

Encouraged, the young mouselet stepped forward. "Hello, gardeners! Could you tell me, please, why you're painting these roses red? They're mousetastically beautiful in white."

Five and Seven both turned to Two.

"The fact is, Miss," Two whispered, "we should have planted a red rosebush here, but we planted a white rosebush by mistake. If the Queen found out, she would cut off all our heads!"

Alice clapped a paw over her snout in HORROR. Moldy mozzarella, how terrible!

"So as you see," Two continued, pointing to the brushes and cans of paint, "we're trying to paint the roses before Her Majesty notices our mistake!"

Just then Five, who was gazing out at the edge of the garden, jumped with surprise.

White Roses, Red Roses

"The Queen is coming! It's the Queeeen!" he shouted.

The three gardeners immediately threw themselves on the ground **snoutdown**.

Alice turned and saw the **strangest** parade she could have ever imagined coming right toward her!

Off with Her Head!

Everyone in the parade was shaped like a playing card! Ten soldiers came first. They were lined up neatly, two by two, carrying **staffs** with clubs on them. Those soldiers were followed by ten playing-card courtiers, also arranged in two lines and adorned with **DIAMONDS**. Behind them were ten royal children, **happy** and carefree, doing graceful **flips** in line.

Then there were the guests, all Kings and Queens of various suits — clubs, diamonds, and spades. Alice recognized the White Rabbit in front of them. He was **fawning** over everyone.

Bringing up the rear of the parade was the

Knave of Hearts. He carried the royal crown on a **VELVET** pillow.

Finally, in marched the King and Queen of Hearts. Double-twisted rattails! Alice had never met real **royalty** before!

The mouselet stood very still and waited for the Queen to reach her.

When the procession came to an **END**, the King and Queen stopped right in front of Alice. Everyone fell silent.

"Who is this?" the Queen of Hearts asked, **glowering**.

The Knave replied with a bow.

"Always bowing, these Knaves. They never do anything else," Her Majesty said drily. "Sometimes I just want a **SIMPLE** answer!"

Then she turned directly to Alice

and asked, "What is your name, young mouse?"

Shaking in her fur, Alice gave a little curtsy and replied politely, "My name is Alice, Your **Royal Majesty**!"

The Queen seemed to approve of this response.

"And who might they be?" she asked, pointing **absentmindedly** at the three gardeners on the ground.

Because they were lying facedown, it was impossible to know which cards they were

 just by looking. For all the Queen knew, they could have been **SOLDIERS**, courtiers, gardeners, or three of her own children!

Alice felt sorry for the poor frightened gardeners, and she decided then and there not to let herself be intimidated. After all, the Queen was just a **playing card**!

"How should I know?" she replied.

The Queen turned **SCARLET** all the way to the points of her crown. "Off with her head! **Off with her head!**" she shouted wildly, motioning for the soldiers to follow her orders.

The King tried to calm her. "Come now, my dear," he whispered. "She's just a little mouselet."

Angrier than a caged cat, the Queen ignored him and walked over to the three cards on the ground.

"Get up!" she commanded.

The gardeners jumped to their paws and started bowing right and left.

"Stop that—you're making me **dizzy**!" the Queen ordered, exasperated.

Looking away from the three gardeners,

the queen noticed the rosebush. Its flowers were now half WHITE and half RED . . . and dripping with paint!

"What is going on here?" she asked threateningly.

Two bowed his head apologetically. "Oh, Your Majesty, we were just trying to—"

"I know exactly what you were trying to do!" the Queen thundered. "Soldiers, *off with their heads*!"

While the Queen's back was turned, the three gardeners ran to Alice for help. *Rats*, she had to do something! She hurried to roll them up and hide them in a nearby flower bed before the Queen spotted them . . .

Do You Know How to Play Croquet?

The Queen suddenly turned around and **smiled**. She took Alice by the arm.

"Do you know how to **play** croquet?" she asked.

"Of course—I love croquet!" Alice squeaked. Before she could twitch a whisker, she was asked to join the procession, right next to the White Rabbit.

"Where is the Duchess?" Alice asked him.

"**Shhhh!**" the Rabbit shushed her, glancing over his shoulder. "You must not squeak of the Duchess for any reason. The Queen has ordered that her head be **chopped off**!"

Alice wasn't surprised. Cheese niblets,

cutting off heads seemed to be the Queen's favorite hobby!

While they were talking, the procession had stopped, and all the cards had arranged themselves for the croquet match.

Alice had never seen such a cheesebrained croquet court! The ground was sprinkled with dips and mounds, the croquet balls were hedgehogs, and the mallets were FLAMINGOS! Plus, to make the wickets, the cards bent over with their paws and feet on the ground.

Alice took her place on the playing field and tried to grab her flamingo, but it wouldn't stay still! Just when she thought she had it straight in her paws, it bent and wiggled all around, tickling her.

Thundering cattails, how frustrating!

The hedgehogs were even worse! When Alice tried to tap one with her mallet, it got up and trotted away. What a mouserific mess!

The whole match was completely confusing. Everyone played at the same time, without waiting for their turn. They kept arguing over which hedgehog was roundest and which rolled the fastest. And the Queen grew enormousely angry every time someone else scored a point. She spent the whole match ordering heads to be chopped off!

Alice had to get out of there! She nervously looked around for a way to escape. As she did, she realized that something was APPEARING in front of her, out of thin air. It looked like . . . a smile!

"Cheese and crackers, the Cheshire

Cat!" Alice cried, happy to see a friendly face amidst all the chaos. (This place really was STRANGE — she never thought she'd be happy to see a **cat**!)

"How are you?" asked the Cat, as soon as his whole mouth had appeared.

It's useless to talk until at least one of his ears appears, Alice thought.

Once the Cat's whole head appeared, Alice explained the situation.

"Do you like the Queen?" the Cat asked.

"Not at all!" Alice confessed.

"Who are you talking to?" the Queen cried when she heard Alice squeaking.

Alice hurried to explain, hoping the Queen hadn't heard what she was saying. "Oh, it's just my friend — the Cheshire Cat!"

"I do not like his face," the King declared,

coming closer. "Get out of here!"

"Off with his head!" the Queen added.

Now Alice had gotten the Cheshire Cat into a mouserific mess!

The King summoned two soldiers who found themselves with a tricky problem: How could they **CUT OFF** the Cat's head if he had no body?

The King, the Queen, and the soldiers discussed the problem for a few minutes, and then turned to Alice. They would let her decide.

Slimy Swiss balls, Alice had to think **FAST** on her paws!

"Well, the Cat belongs to the Duchess," Alice pointed out. "Maybe you should ask her."

The Queen considered this advice. "Very

well," she agreed. "The Duchess is in **prison**. Soldiers, bring her here at once!"

The soldiers sprang into action, like mice on a cheese hunt. But as soon as they left, the Cheshire Cat's head began to **vanish**.

By the time the soldiers returned with the Duchess, the Cheshire Cat had disappeared without a trace!

The Moral is . . .

As soon as the Duchess spotted Alice, she **JOYFULLY** grabbed her paw.

"Oh, it's so *fabumouse* to see you, my dear old friend!" she cried with an affectionate smile.

Holey cheese, how **strange**! At least she was in a **good mood**. Maybe when Alice had met the Duchess in the kitchen, she had been irritated by all that pepper . . .

It must be a worthy scientific experiment, Alice thought. **PEPPER** *makes one irritable, just like sugar makes one sweet. Oh, if only scientists realized that! Pepper would be banned from every kitchen in the world, and there would be far fewer arguments!*

The Moral Is . . .

Lost in her thoughts, Alice forgot all about the Duchess. When she **heard** the Duchess's voice again, she nearly *jumped* out of her fur!

"You're thinking about something, dear," the Duchess observed, "so you forgot to squeak. And the moral here is . . . well, I don't know, but I'll think of it soon."

"Maybe there isn't a moral," Alice suggested.

"Don't make *jokes*, little one!" the Duchess scolded her. "There's a moral in everything, you know. One just needs to find it."

Meanwhile, the croquet match had started up again. All the players on the field had grabbed their **flamingos**.

"Now that the flamingos are cooperating, the **game** will go much better," Alice said.

"Yes!" the Duchess agreed heartily. "And the moral there is: Love is what makes the world TURN!"

Alice scratched her snout. Cheesy cream puffs, what was she squeaking about?

The Duchess went on, "Your flamingo looks a little NERVOUS."

Alice shrugged. "I don't think so, but it's better not to bother him. He could bite us—"

"Bite!" the Duchess **cried**. "Just like mustard—it has bite, too. And the moral there is: Birds of a feather flock together!"

PUTRID CHEESE PUFFS! That made no sense at all—mustard wasn't a bird!

Suddenly, the Duchess grew whiter than a ball of mozzarella. The Queen was heading right for them, and she had a **menacing** look on her snout!

"You have two choices," the Queen thundered at the Duchess, stomping her paw. "Either **you** disappear, or **YoUR HEAD** disappears!"

The Duchess scurried away **immediately**.

"Excellent," the Queen said, rubbing her paws together. "Now we can continue the match."

Alice was squeakless! **Terrified**, she followed the Queen onto the croquet court.

The Lazy Gryphon

While the Queen had been dealing with the Duchess, the croquet players had all decided to take a nap. Now they rushed back onto the field, RUBBING their eyes.

The Queen continued the game as before, *shouting*, "Off with his head!" and "Off with her head!" carelessly. By the time the match was halfway over, everyone except the King, Alice, and the Queen had been taken into **custody** by the guards. How **fur-raising**!

At that point, the Queen declared the end of the match. She took Alice aside. "Have you *seen* the Mock Turtle?" she asked.

Alice shook her snout. She had no clue

what the Queen was even squeaking about!

"Well, you must meet him immediately," the Queen replied. "Follow me!"

As they left, Alice heard the King whisper to the prisoners, "Everyone is **PARDONED**! Shhh . . ."

Alice tried not to let the Queen see the **smile** on her snout!

After a short walk, Alice and the Queen reached a large **Gryphon**, fast asleep on the beach.

"Get up, lazybones!" the Queen cried, tugging on his tail.

Putrid cheese puffs— Alice had never seen a creature like this before! The back half of the Gryphon's body was a lion, and the front half

was an eagle with enormouse wings and a sharp **BEAK**. Alice was shaking in her fur just looking at him!

The Gryphon **struggled** to sit up, rubbing his sleepy eyes.

"You're always sleeping!" the Queen reproached him. "Take this young mouselet to the Mock Turtle. I have a dozen prisoners waiting for me!"

Alice felt her whiskers wobble, but she tried to be **BRAVE**. The Gryphon didn't look very NICE, but she figured she would be safer with him than with the Queen!

The Sad, Sad Story of the Mock Turtle

As soon as the Queen left, the Gryphon **STRETCHED** and looked at Alice.

"Come with me," he said, **SHAKING** his wings.

"My goodness," Alice grumbled, careful not to be overheard. "'Come with me this way!' 'Come with me that way!' I've never received so many orders in my whole life."

After a short walk, they spotted a large **TURTLE** . . . with the head of a cow! It was sitting on the beach alone, sobbing. Cheese niblets, Alice thought her **HEART** might break!

The Sad, Sad Story of the Mock Turtle

"Mock Turtle," the Gryphon began, "this young mouselet has come to hear your STORY!"

The Turtle blew his nose and looked at Alice with teary **eyes**.

"As you wish," he agreed, sniffling. "But you must stay seated until the end!"

Alice and the Gryphon sat quietly and listened to the *sniff, sniff* of the inconsolable Turtle for several minutes.

I don't see how we can stay seated until the **end***, Alice thought, if he doesn't even* **start** *telling his story!*

But just then the Mock Turtle spoke up. "Once, I was a True Turtle."

These solemn words were followed by a VERY LONG silence. After a while, Alice was just about to get up, thank the Mock Turtle for the interesting story, and leave.

"When we were little," the Turtle finally continued, "we went to school in the sea. Our teacher was a **true** turtle. We called him Tortoise."

"Why did you call him Tortoise if he was a turtle?" Alice asked, confused.

"We called him Tortoise because he **taught us**, and that sounds like 'Tortoise,'" the Turtle explained, as if that was obvious. He **squeezed** his eyes shut so tightly that tears flew everywhere. "Anyway, we went to **SCHOOL** in the sea every single weekday."

Alice couldn't resist commenting. "Well, I go to school every weekday, too . . ."

"Do you also study lots of subjects?" the Turtle asked, sounding nervous.

"Of course!" Alice replied. "Things like French and music."

"And laundry?" the Turtle asked.

Alice shook her snout. "No, not laundry."

"Then it's not a **good** school!" the Turtle declared, relieved.

Double-twisted rattails, this was taking forever! And it didn't make much sense. All the same, Alice couldn't help feeling **curious**.

"What else were you taught in school?" she asked.

"Well, there was wave theory, both ancient and modern," the Turtle explained, counting the subjects on his feet, "with courses in foam studies. Oh, and a class in slithering —"

"But how did they teach those things?" Alice asked, more curious than ever.

The Sad, Sad Story of the Mock Turtle

"I don't know!" the Turtle moaned, bursting into tears again. "I only took the most **BASIC** classes."

"And I didn't have any time to study!" the Gryphon added with a sigh.

The pair exchanged sympathetic looks.

Finally, the Gryphon shook himself and sat up tall. "**Cheer up**, Turtle! Can you tell us about some sea games, instead?"

The Lobsters' Quadrille

The Mock Turtle **SIGHED** for the hundredth time and wiped his eyes.

"Well, if you want to know a very funny *game* from the sea," he said to Alice, "you have to learn the lobsters' quadrille!"

"It's a very well-known **DANCE**," the Gryphon added, getting excited.

The Turtle and the Gryphon began to take turns describing the dance very enthusiastically.

Soon, Alice found herself turning from right to left and left to right over and over and over again, as if she were watching a game of PING-PONG!

"To begin, the dancers must form

156

a long line along the edge of the sea," the Gryphon said.

"Two lines!" the Turtle corrected him. "With sharks, octopuses, sea horses, and other fish. Then you have to separate all the **JELLYFISH**."

"This takes a long time!" the Gryphon explained.

The Turtle nodded. "And then everyone takes two steps **forward** . . ."

"Each paired with a lobster!"

"Then you stand facing one another . . ."

"And switch lobsters, and take two steps **BACK**!"

"Yes! And then everyone throws their lobsters . . ."

"Into the air!" the Gryphon

shouted, leaping into the air to demonstrate. "As FAR out to sea as possible . . ."

"And then swims after them!"

"And does SOMERSAULTS in the water!" the Turtle cried.

"Yessss!" The Gryphon clapped excitedly. "Then they switch lobsters again!"

"And go back to the water's edge, and—"

The Mock Turtle suddenly got quiet again.

"Those are the first steps," he concluded.

The two creatures had been jumping around throughout the whole story, but now they sat down quietly, looking sad. Rats, it seemed like Alice would never figure these two out!

"It sounds like a fabumouse dance," she

squeaked timidly, trying not to upset them any further.

The Mock Turtle's teary face suddenly **lit up**. "Would you like to see it?"

Alice smiled. "Oh, I'd like that very much!"

"Let's try the first steps!" the Turtle **cried**, gesturing for the Gryphon to join him. "We don't have lobsters, but they're not absolutely necessary."

Alice *twisted her whiskers* — no lobsters in the lobsters' quadrille? Thundering cattails, how **SiLLy**!

But before she could reply, the Mock Turtle and the Gryphon started to dance **clumsily** around her, stepping on her paws when they got too close.

If they keep this up, my paws will be **pulverized**! Alice thought.

As they **danced**, the Turtle bellowed

a song to accompany them. Alice tried to understand it, but she was so busy protecting her paws that she could only make out something about a codfish.

A lobsters' quadrille without lobsters and a SONG *about codfish?* Alice thought. *I must have missed something — this is the most* cheesebrained *thing I've ever heard!*

Codfish, Sea Shiners, and Shoes in the Sea

At the end of the dance, Alice clapped politely. Careful that the Gryphon and the Mock Turtle wouldn't notice, she **PEEKED** down at her paws. Luckily, they were still in one piece after being stepped on so many times. **Whew!**

"Bravo!" she said. "That was a very, um, **graceful** dance. And I really enjoyed the song about the codfish, too! Though I'm not sure I completely **understood** it . . ."

"Oh, speaking of codfish," the Mock Turtle replied, still trying to catch his breath, "you've seen them before, right?"

Alice nodded, thinking about codfish she'd

164

seen served in restaurants. "Yes, though the ones I've seen have their tails stuffed in their mouths, and they're covered with bread crumbs!"

The Turtle shook his head, indignant. "Bread crumbs? No, bread crumbs would get **WASHED AWAY** in the sea! Though they do often have their tails in their mouths. Do you know why? It's actually very **interesting** . . ."

Just then the Mock Turtle suddenly yawned and fell asleep, exhausted from all his wild dancing.

The Gryphon picked up where the Turtle had left off, lowering his voice so he wouldn't wake his friend. "One day, the codfish wanted to go to the ball with the lobsters, so they flung themselves into the sea and let the current carry them to the ball. They held their tails tightly in their mouths so they wouldn't accidentally swim out of the current. But by the time they reached the ball, none of the codfish could get their tails out of their mouths!"

Cheese and crackers, Alice had never heard so much about codfish in her life!

"And that's not all!" the Gryphon continued, nodding with authority. "Do you know why codfish are so shiny? Do you know what's used to shine your shoes?"

Alice was confused—which question was she supposed to answer? And what did her shoes have to do with anything?

She examined her shoes. "Well, my parents use shoe shine on my shoes, I think . . ."

"That's right!" the Gryphon said.

166

"Shoe shine is used on land. But at the bottom of the sea, boots and shoes are shined with codfish. That's why they're called *sea shiners*!"

Alice had never heard of sea shiners, but she had to admit, they sounded interesting.

"What are shoes made of at the bottom of the sea?" she asked, twisting her tail thoughtfully and trying to figure out why sea creatures would even need shoes.

"They have soles made of sole, and eels for shoelaces, of course," the Gryphon replied, snapping his **beak** impatiently. "Everyone knows that! Now it's your turn! Tell us about one of your adventures."

"Yes, yes!" added the Turtle, waking up and yawning.

"Well, I can tell you about the adventure that began yesterday," Alice said, smoothing her fur. "So much has happened since then! I was a whole different mouse . . ."

Alice began to tell them about her extraordinary DaY, starting when she spotted the White Rabbit. At first, she was a little nervous—the Gryphon and Turtle looked awfully serious as they listened! But she grew more confident as the story went on. She described everything that had happened to her in great detail. When she got to the part about the Caterpillar, the Turtle JUMPED. "A Caterpillar on a mushroom? How curious!"

"It's all very curious, as curious as can be," the Gryphon declared gravely.

Just then shouts rang through the air.

"The trial! The trial!"

Codfish, Sea Shiners, and Shoes in the Sea

Before Alice could ask what was going on, the Gryphon grabbed her paw and started to **RUN** in the direction of the shouting, leaving the slow Mock Turtle behind.

"What trial?" asked Alice as she scrambled to keep up.

But the Gryphon didn't reply—he just **RAN** faster and faster . . .

Who Stole the Tarts?

Before Alice and the Gryphon knew it, they found themselves right in the middle of some kind of COURTROOM.

Looking around, Alice saw that the King and the Queen were presiding over the room, seated on their **thrones**. A great crowd of **birds** and other creatures had gathered around them, along with a full suit of Hearts. Before the King and Queen stood the Knave of Hearts, chained up and guarded by two soldiers.

The White Rabbit, dressed in uniform, oversaw the proceedings. He sat on a swing next to the King, with a **trumpet** in one paw and a roll of parchment in the other.

Who Stole the Tarts?

In the middle of the room was a table with a large plate piled high with cream cheese **TARTS**. Alice's mouth started watering. They looked whisker-licking good!

Alice had never been in a courtroom before, but she had read many descriptions in books and remembered what things were called.

He's the judge, she thought, looking at the King. *I recognize the* wig.

Even though he was wearing his crown on top of a gigantic curly wig, the King looked mousetastically out of place. He didn't seem comfortable at all!

Those twelve creatures holding **notepads** *must be the jurors. Oh, look! There's Bill the Lizard!*

Alice was very proud of how **much** she knew!

Who Stole the Tarts?

The twelve jurors were all busy scribbling on their notepads with pencils.

"What are they **writing**?" Alice whispered to the Gryphon. "They can't take notes—the trial hasn't even **started** yet!"

"They're writing their names," the Gryphon replied quietly. "I imagine they're afraid of **forgetting** them before the trial is over."

"Oh, how **SILLY**!" Alice squeaked with a laugh. Right away, she saw the jurors all writing "How silly!" on their notepads.

"Oops," Alice muttered under her breath. She'd have to stay **quiet as a mouse** from then on!

"Shhhh! Silence in the courtroom!" the White Rabbit hollered, **GLARING**.

In the silence, Alice noticed Bill the Lizard's pencil was squeaking. Rats! She couldn't stand the sound of a squeaky pencil!

So she quietly slipped behind Bill and, quick as a mouse on a cheese hunt, grabbed his pencil. The Lizard didn't notice a thing! He calmly continued writing on his blank notepad with his finger. Alice clapped a paw over her mouth to keep from giggling.

At that point, the King got to his paws. "Chancellor! Read the charges!" he ordered the White Rabbit.

The Rabbit played three long blasts on his trumpet: *TOOOOT, TOOOOT, TOOOOOOOOOT!*

Then he unrolled the parchment in his paw and read, "This morning, Her Royal and Imperial Majesty, Our Sovereign Queen of Hearts, prepared a dish of delicious

royal cream cheese tarts." He **paused** and nodded toward the plate on the table. "This afternoon, the evil Knave of Hearts stole the aforementioned tarts, thereby committing an outrageous **offense** against Her Majesty—"

"That's enough!" the King interrupted, **impatient** and ready to move things along. He turned to the jury and said, "Now, good jurors, write down your **VERDICT**!"

"**NO! NO!**" the Rabbit intervened, holding up a paw in alarm. "First, we must call the witnesses!"

The King tugged at his whiskers, embarrassed. "Of course, of course," he said, clearing his throat. "The **WITNESSES**!

What did I say? Please call . . . um . . . the first witness, whoever it is!"

Satisfied, the Rabbit gave another three blasts on his trumpet and announced, "First witness in the courtroom!"

Order! Order!

The first witness was none other than the *MAD HATTER*!

He presented himself to the King and Queen with a CUP of tea in one paw and a piece of buttered toast in the other. The March Hare and the Dormouse followed him in, **arm in arm**.

"Pardon me for eating a little *snack*, Your Highnesses," the Hatter said. "I hadn't finished my tea when I was called!"

"**Teatime** is long over," the King scolded. "When did you start?"

The Hatter looked at the March Hare. "The fourteenth of March, I think?"

"Fifteenth," the Hare corrected him.

Order! Order!

"Sixteenth," the Dormouse interrupted.

The King listened thoughtfully and then turned to the jurors. "That's an important detail, jurors! VERY IMPORTANT!"

The jurors all carefully wrote down the three dates.

The King turned back to the Hatter. "Take off your hat," he ordered.

"Oh, but it's not mine," the Hatter said.

"Then you StoLe it!" the King declared, looking over at the jury to make sure they were listening.

The Hatter held up his paws. "No, no! I sell hats. I am a Hatter!"

The Queen hadn't seemed to care much about the Hatter, but now she stared intensely at him.

Order! Order!

The Hatter turned as pale as a mozzarella milkshake.

Just then Alice began to feel STRANGE. *Crusty cat litter — I feel heavier!* she thought. *But I haven't eaten anything!*

Looking around, she realized that she was growing again — and fast!

"Hey, you're squishing me!" the Dormouse complained.

"I'm so sorry, but I can't help it!" Alice squeaked.

"WAIT!" the Queen cried, still studying the Hatter. "Someone bring me the list of the singers from the last concert!"

Uh-oh, Alice thought. *She must remember the Hatter's horrible rendition of "Twinkle, Twinkle!" Rancid ricotta!*

At this, the Hatter's knees trembled. He was so nervous that he took a big bite out of his teacup rather than his BUTTERED toast!

Then, terrified, he threw himself at the King's feet.

"Oh, Sire! I am just a poor Hatter who drinks tea — just ask the Hare!"

The March Hare shook his head. "I deny it!"

"He **DENiES** it!" the King repeated. "Jurors, overlook that part."

At this point, a guinea pig seated in the jury cheered and applauded. In the twitch of a tail, two guards STUFFED him into a canvas sack, tied it with twine, and sat on top of it.

Holey cheese!

Distracted by the interruption, the King dismissed the Hatter. The Hatter *ran off* in a hurry!

Order! Order!

The next witness was the Duchess's cook, who entered the courtroom holding a huge **pepper grinder**. As she stepped forward, everyone in the room started sneezing.

Achoo! Achoo! A-a-achoo!

The King ignored the sneezes and continued the interrogation, knitting his brows together **sternly** so that he would look intimidating. "First of all, what were the tarts made of?"

"**Pepper!**" the cook replied.

"Cream cheese," a sleepy little voice corrected her.

Everyone turned to see who had spoken. It was the Dormouse!

The Queen, who was still reading the list of singers she'd requested earlier, looked **UP**.

Order! Order!

"Arrest that Dormouse!" she roared. "Pull out his whiskers! Off with his head!"

The whole room turned to **CHAOS** as everyone tried to capture the Dormouse, who was scampering and **JUMPING** around frantically.

"Order! Order!" the White Rabbit **hollered**, using the trumpet as a megaphone and trying to get everyone settled in their seats again.

Finally, after some time, the Dormouse was kicked out of the courtroom. Rat-munching rattlesnakes, how **ridiculous**!

Alice didn't know much about the law, but she knew enough to understand that this courtroom was outrageous.

Once everything settled down, Alice noticed that the Duchess's cook had

disappeared.

"It doesn't matter," said the King, tugging on his whiskers. "Call the final witness!"

The frazzled White Rabbit consulted the list of witnesses, **unrolling** it until he reached the last line. Then he announced, "The court calls to the stand . . . Alice!"

Alice Takes the Stand

At the sound of her name, Alice flinched. **Rats!** She was being called as a witness?

"**Here!**" she shouted.

Then, forgetting that she had grown **ENORMOUSE**, she jumped to her paws and accidentally covered the jury box with the hem of her skirt. All the jurors *scrambled* out of the way, yelping in surprise and tossing their notepads and pencils into the AIR.

"Oh, excuse me!" Alice cried, **MORTIFIED**. She frantically gathered up the jurors and put them back in their places one by one.

The King and the Queen watched with **WIDE EYES**.

"The trial cannot continue until all the jurors are seated!" the King declared gravely.

Alice struggled to hurry up and put everyone where they had been before. But just when she thought the jurors were all back in place . . .

"I mean **EVERYONE!**" the King boomed.

Alice followed his sharp gaze. Moldy mozzarella—in her hurry, she had placed Bill **upside down**! Now the poor lizard's tail was waving around in the air. Alice turned him right side up, then gave each juror his notepad and pencil back.

As soon as the jurors had recovered, they all started scribbling on their notepads. One drew flowers, another filled a page with curlicues, and another carefully counted the pencils still on the courtroom floor and wrote down ZERO.

Alice Takes the Stand

They were all writing except for Bill, who still seemed so **shaken** that he couldn't do anything but sit with his mouth open and his tongue hanging out.

The King finally began Alice's **interrogation**. This was quite different than the earlier interrogations, because this time the witness was much **BIGGER** than any other creature there!

"Well," the King began, sitting up straight to appear a bit **TALLER**, "what do you know about the stolen tarts?"

"Nothing," Alice replied with a shrug.

"**NOTHING** at all?" the King pressed.

"Nothing at all," Alice confirmed.

"That is very **important**!"

the King declared, turning to the jury box.

"You mean *unimportant*, Your Majesty!" the White Rabbit said.

The King nodded, making all the *curls* on his wig bounce. "Of course, of course! Unimportant! What did I say?"

Then the King repeated, "Important, unimportant, important, unimportant," to himself, trying to figure out which word sounded better.

Alice **rolled** her giant eyes.

Then she watched as someone in the jury wrote "***important***" on his notepad, someone else wrote "*unimportant*," and someone else wrote both words.

The King spent a few minutes in ***silence***, lost in his thoughts. Then he opened his royal ledger and wrote something down, **nodding** with satisfaction every time he

finished a line. When he stopped writing, he **solemnly** gestured for silence.

"Listen, everyone!" he ordered.

The courtroom was silent — no one dared to **squeak**!

Rule Forty-Two

The King cleared his throat and read from his ledger: "Rule forty-two: Every person taller than four thousand feet must leave the hall."

All eyes turned to Alice.

"I'm not taller than four thousand feet!" she said indignantly.

The King looked her up and down, trying to judge her height. "I'd say you're EXACTLY that tall!"

"More like six thousand feet," the Queen corrected him.

"Well it doesn't matter, because I'm not leaving!" Alice said. "Plus, that's not even a real RULE — you just invented it!"

Rule Forty-Two

The King shook his head. "You wouldn't know, but this is the oldest rule in the royal ledger!"

"If it's the oldest, then it should be rule one, not forty-two!" Alice pointed out.

The King turned as pale as a slab of mozzarella and slammed his ledger shut before anyone could take a PEEK at it. Then he turned to the jury and murmured, "Um, write down the verdict . . ."

"But, Your Majesty!" the White Rabbit cried, frustrated. "We're not done with some important testimony! Plus, someone just delivered this message."

The Rabbit held a folded piece of paper in one paw. "It seems to be a message from the prisoner to someone!"

"Yes, that makes sense," the King agreed. "After all, it couldn't be a letter written to

no one. That would be awfully strange."

The White Rabbit nodded and read the message. "It's not a letter," he reported. "It's a poem."

"But is it written in the prisoner's pawwriting?" asked a juror.

The Rabbit squinted at the paper.

"No," he finally replied. "And *that* is the STRANGEST thing."

All the jurors were baffled by this revelation. They couldn't think of a single explanation!

"Maybe the prisoner imitated someone else's pawwriting," the King suggested.

At that point, the Knave of Hearts finally stepped forward. "Your Majesty," he said in despair, "I assure you that I never wrote that message! See? I didn't sign it."

"If you didn't sign it," the King said

disapprovingly, "it's even worse! That shows your dishonesty! If you had good intentions, you would have signed your name like any *honest* creature!"

Holey cheese — that may have been the first intelligent thing the King had said all day!

"But what does the poem say?" one of the jurors asked.

The Rabbit folded up the paper and scratched one of his ears. "I don't know."

For the love of all things cheesy, this was the most CONFUSING trial Alice could imagine!

"**Very well!**" the King said. "This is the most important piece of proof we've seen. The jury can now write down their verdict!"

"No, no, no!" the Queen interrupted.

Rule Forty-Two

"First the sentence, then the verdict."

"Do you all have **cheese** for brains?!" Alice cried. She felt like tearing out her whiskers!

The Queen spun to look at her. "**HOW DARE YOU?** Off with her head!"

The whole pack of cards launched themselves at the young mouselet. Rancid ricotta, she was in trouble now!

"Paws off!" Alice squeaked. "**Help! Help!**"

Alice, Wake Up!

As she flailed wildly to defend herself against the cards, Alice heard a voice calling her from far away. "Alice! Alice! Alice!"

Who was that? Maybe she was just imagining things . . .

"Alice, WAKE UP!"

Alice half opened her eyes. Cheesy cream puffs, how strange! She was lying on something soft. Even stranger, the cards had suddenly disappeared, and everything around her was peaceful . . .

"You've slept for so long!" the voice squeaked.

Alice sat up and saw her sister!

"Oh!" she cried, still a bit sleepy. "I had a **very strange** dream!"

She immediately started to recount her fabumouse **adventures**, trying to remember every curious detail.

Her sister listened with a big smile on her snout. "What an **imagination**!" she said when Alice had finished. She grabbed Alice's paw and pulled her up. "Now let's go home! It's time for tea."

Alice nodded, following her sister across the garden. As they walked, her sister admired the beautiful **sunset**. Suddenly, she imagined all the creatures Alice had told her about coming to life right in front of her!

She saw the **grass** rustle from the White Rabbit's paws and smelled the **SHORE** where Alice had met the Dodo. She heard the sound of the Mad Hatter's teacups clinking together, the heavy **breathing** of the sleepy Dormouse, the screams of the Queen of Hearts, the Duchess's **sneezes**, the Mock Turtle's sobs . . .

And she imagined little Alice growing up, but still dreaming about worlds full of marvemouse **wonders** that she could share with other curious and imaginative young mouselets!

Lewis Carroll

ewis Carroll (his real name was Charles Lutwidge Dodgson) was a great English writer, mathematician, and photographer.

He was born in Daresbury, England, in 1832. He was shy but quickly proved himself to be excellent at mathematics. He loved numbers, but he also loved words! Even as a child, he wrote poetry and told stories to his ten siblings.

Carroll suffered from a stutter, but was

an excellent storyteller all the same. He was especially good at entertaining children with riddles and wordplay!

He was appointed as a professor of mathematics at Oxford University, and became friends with its dean, Henry Liddell. During a picnic, Carroll told one of the dean's daughters, Alice, the story of a curious little girl who had a strange adventure. Alice Liddell loved the story so much that she begged him to write it down so she wouldn't forget it! So *Alice's Adventures in Wonderland* was born, followed by *Through the Looking-Glass*. The novels were a great success, and continue to enchant readers of all ages today!

Lewis Carroll died of pneumonia in 1898, at the age of sixty-five, in Guildford, England.

ABOUT THE AUTHOR

 Born in New Mouse City, Mouse Island, **GERONIMO STILTON** is Rattus Emeritus of Mousomorphic Literature and of Neo-Ratonic Comparative Philosophy. For the past twenty years, he has been running *The Rodent's Gazette*, New Mouse City's most widely read daily newspaper.

Stilton was awarded the Ratitzer Prize for his scoops on *The Curse of the Cheese Pyramid* and *The Search for Sunken Treasure*. He has also received the Andersen 2000 Prize for Personality of the Year. One of his bestsellers won the 2002 eBook Award for world's best ratlings' electronic book. His works have been published all over the globe.

In his spare time, Mr. Stilton collects antique cheese rinds and plays golf. But what he most enjoys is telling stories to his nephew Benjamin.

Don't miss any of these exciting Thea Sisters adventures!

Thea Stilton and the Dragon's Code

Thea Stilton and the Mountain of Fire

Thea Stilton and the Ghost of the Shipwreck

Thea Stilton and the Secret City

Thea Stilton and the Mystery in Paris

Thea Stilton and the Cherry Blossom Adventure

Thea Stilton and the Star Castaways

Thea Stilton: Big Trouble in the Big Apple

Thea Stilton and the Ice Treasure

Thea Stilton and the Secret of the Old Castle

Thea Stilton and the Blue Scarab Hunt

Thea Stilton and the Prince's Emerald

Thea Stilton and the Mystery on the Orient Express

Thea Stilton and the Dancing Shadows

Thea Stilton and the Legend of the Fire Flowers

Thea Stilton and the Spanish Dance Mission

Thea Stilton and the Journey to the Lion's Den

**Thea Stilton and the
Great Tulip Heist**

**Thea Stilton and the
Chocolate Sabotage**

**Thea Stilton and the
Missing Myth**

**Thea Stilton and the
Lost Letters**

**Thea Stilton and the
Tropical Treasure**

**Thea Stilton and the
Hollywood Hoax**

**Thea Stilton and the
Madagascar Madness**

Up Next!

**Thea Stilton and the
Frozen Fiasco**

And check out my fabumouse special editions!

**THEA STILTON:
THE JOURNEY
TO ATLANTIS**

**THEA STILTON:
THE SECRET OF
THE FAIRIES**

**THEA STILTON:
THE SECRET OF
THE SNOW**

**THEA STILTON:
THE CLOUD
CASTLE**

**THEA STILTON:
THE TREASURE
OF THE SEA**

Dear mouse friends,
Thanks for reading, and farewell
till the next book.
It'll be another whisker-licking-good
adventure, and that's a promise!

Geronimo Stilton